one dater theory

one dater theory

kelby gansel

Tate Publishing & *Enterprises*

One Dater Theory

This title is also available as a Tate Out Loud product. Visit www.tatepublishing.com for more information.

This novel is a work of fiction. However, several names, descriptions, entities and incidents included in the story are based on the lives of real people.

The opinions expressed by the author are not necessarily those of Tate Publishing, LLC.

Published by Tate Publishing & Enterprises, LLC
127 E. Trade Center Terrace | Mustang, Oklahoma 73064 USA
1.888.361.9473 | www.tatepublishing.com

Tate Publishing is committed to excellence in the publishing industry. The company reflects the philosophy established by the founders, based on Psalms 68:11,
"The Lord gave the word and great was the company of those who published it."

Cover design by Lynly Taylor
Interior design by Brandon Wood
Published in the United States of America

ISBN: 978-1-60247-742-1
1. Fiction/Contemporary Dating

07.10.16

the beginning

As a child my mother always told me I was beautiful and that one day my prince charming would come and we would live happily ever after. But what else are you to believe at the age of twelve? That's when I realized that in the 21st century meeting a man could not only be difficult and challenging but that choosing a pair of shoes to wear with an evening outfit could be easy as pie. I sometimes laugh at what has happened to the dating scene because it seems everyone is looking for love but in my case love has left me to wonder why I am still single and why can't those fairy tale endings still exist.

Being single in New York City, a place that houses thousands upon millions of single people, is not all it's cracked up to be. Dating is still hard regardless of if the city you live in is rated number five on the best places to live if you are single. I mean just because you live in a city where your chances of finding that perfect someone out weigh the male to female ratio means absolutely nothing in today's dating age. It's amazing when you start to think about how the world is almost obsessed with finding that perfect someone. I mean, we even had dating shows that go back to the early seventies that try to succeed where we have failed. Today you can turn on the television and see just about ten different dating shows that really ask the question: where are all the good looking, honest, hardworking, and decent single people? Honestly have you ever watched the Bachelor or Bachelorette and sat there asking yourself, Where did they find such great looking people who actually have the qualities I have been searching for in another individual? Well I did. I was watching the second episode of the Bachelorette. I sat there in my pajamas on my sofa thinking about how this girl on the show was no different from me. She was pretty, smart, fun and searching for love. And then there were sixteen or more good-looking guys from all over the United States searching for love. I sat there thinking, Why am I still single? But then I remembered it's television and until they (the people on the show) step into reality everything will seem like a dream.

I believe the dating scene is comprised of men and women searching for that connection, that indescribable feeling when two people meet for the first time, that spark or instantaneous power that brings two willing bodies into a trance where the world around them disappears. I know it sounds like something that a movie or a romantic novel would depict but I am telling you the dating scene has gone crazy. With everything from dating services to the Internet to prearranged marriages to blind dates or just leaving things up to fate, everyone wants the same thing...Love. The question is how to find love and figuring out if love really exists especially with so many people settling for something less than perfect. An uncle of mine once told me, "Kelby, do not settle for any man." Of course I sat there and listened to his speech but then again all this was coming from a man who had been married five times and had two affairs during his lifetime.

I am sorry but I don't think I introduced myself. Where are my manners? I do apolize. My name is Kelby Smith and I have been unsuccessful in finding someone to love. So this is my story. I live in the big apple and what a better place to meet someone and start a business. I attended NYU and the best part about living in the city is that most of my friends live right here, which is great. It's just that my friends and even my family really have no clue to what I want in another individual. Between you and me, the list has gotten shorter over the years. Honestly, right now, all I want is someone who is decent. And even that is stretching it but all will be explained, I promise.

I studied Psychology and I opened a small private practice in the West Village right off of Blecker Street. When you own your business, you rarely get an opportunity to meet new people and when you own a practice the last thing you want to do is date one of your patients. Trust me I know.

So here I am on a Saturday evening dateless wondering what is it that men want. I start to question the impossible and with a sip of wine I was out for the evening.

See I have a theory that I have indeed become a "one dater" as I like to put it. Let me explain. In the dating world everyone has expectations of what Mr. Right or Miss Right would be like. Guys usually say they want a woman who is independent, career driver, witty, intelligent, and beautiful. Women usually say they want a man who is goal orientated, smart, compassionate, has a good job and handsome. Now these are all perfectly normal expectations for anyone to want in another individual. But what happens when you meet someone who represents all those qualities and more? Do you take a chance and see what can happen? Or do run in the opposite direction? See, my theory had developed based upon my own dating experiences and why men do not seem to be interested in someone who portrays all the qualities they have ever wanted in the opposite sex.

We all have been there, in that horrible place called the dating world and we all have experienced the worst. Now all the women who read this will agree that it's hard to be a strong professional woman in today's world because the men today are not ready for an independent woman. If men really were ready for an independent woman then I would not be single. At least I would like to think so. Now I am not saying that I am bitter about what has been happening over these last past months. It just becomes frustrating at times because you are constantly wondering, Is it me? You become super critical about who you are, your body image, how you interact with others and then finally you start analyzing your inner-self that soon you feel as if you are going mad.

Luckily, I have not reached that point in my life where you dig into your subconscious looking at your childhood and seeing how it effects your relationships with the opposite sex. Since I describe myself as a strong woman it would not be wise for me to inform the world that I am unstable or that I have some mental imbalance. This of course is not true but I will tell you this, exercise has become my new form of therapy.

You are probably wondering what is this "one dater" theory all about. Well, I was just about to explain how it all works. Let's begin with the introduction. Let's say you meet someone whether it's through family, friends, Internet dating or just by chance. So you begin to talk to each other maybe for a couple days via phone or email especially if you have not met them in person. Things start going well during those first couple of days. There's good conversation. There's witty banter. There's a common connection.

Then someone proposes that a meeting should take place. You say, "Fine, I have no problem with meeting people. This will be fun." Now if the individual you are meeting has never seen you before but only heard the sound of your voice then in their mind they have created an image based upon a verbal or written description of what you might look like. So there becomes a sense of mystery and curiosity that occurs in their minds. The curiosity leads them into a world of unknown certainty where fantasy and reality become two complete opposites from what they originally mean.

A perfect example of what I speak of comes into play when you use the Internet as a way of meeting people. Now there's nothing wrong with Internet dating it's just that the guys you meet through the Internet tend to have their own ideas about what Miss Right should look like. These men are what I like to call "the dreamers." They scroll the Internet reading about each woman and viewing their picture to see if there is an instant of goose bump that takes place. But it's when they come across a profile (a brief description of the person and what their ideal match would be or what they are looking for in the opposite sex) where there is no picture attached, that's when they begin to wonder. They start to create an image in their head. They develop a fantasy woman; a woman that is perfection. You know what I mean; a woman that can be silly and sexy at the same time. A woman who can walk through a room gracefully where everyone stops to stare as a silent whisper fills the room.

So here I am trying something new, Internet dating, that is. Like all of us who have been out there in the dating world, we begin to get tried of the same old pick up lines and guys acting like someone that just step out of a GQ magazine. And after spending years at the bars and clubs, meeting all the wrong men possible under sun, I figured what's the harm in changing the way I meet people. So I began to scan through the Internet sites seeing what it all was about. Scrolling through profile after profile reading what all these other singles had to say. So I picked a site to begin my new adventure. Let me share with you what I had written about myself on this particular Internet site:

> Have you ever wondered what Ms. Right would look like? Well, I have been wondering what Mr. Right would look like and then it occurred to me that it doesn't matter what he really looks like. Over the years I have been looking closer at the people I see on the street with their special someone by their side. And said to myself, "She not beautiful but he is or he's not beautiful but she is." Then asked that same old question, "What is it about the one person that makes the other so happy inside that they could not picture themselves without the other?" When I look in the mirror I do not see perfection; just a cute little blonde with a petite body who can make people happy with her smile.
>
> I have been looking for that special someone, but today who hasn't? I have always said to myself that one day when my career is on track, a great person will come into my life. Well, here I am and I'm a therapist practicing in New York and feeling excited about what lays ahead. I do not play games because honestly I do not have time for that because there is a whole world awaiting me. Well boys, I am cute, funny, outgoing, smart, into the arts and theater and most of all I love New York City. So do not waste another minute thinking about if you should write me, just do it!

Not bad right? It has some appeal to it. It's creative

and witty just like me. And obviously I started to attract people or at least making them a little bit curious. So where did I go wrong with men? Why did all the men, after reading something like that, feel the need to run instead of giving me a chance so they could get to know me better? But wait a minute, I am jumping the gun here. You will begin to understand more of what I mean as we continue to go on and how this theory fits the story of the life I've had for the last past few months.

Now before you start thinking that I am some wacky thirty-two year old girl from Greenwich, Connecticut I will have you know that I am just a simple but cute/adorable blonde who just wants a little romance. There is this picture on my apartment wall in the living room. It is a classic example of two people who feel nothing but love, true love for one another. There in the picture you see a nineteen forties train in the background with the smoke coming over the front part of the train. The man is standing on the train platform and his love is in his arms. And they are savoring this kiss. Now you do not know if this kiss is a goodbye kiss or "I have been away so long" kiss.

Now I will tell you that if you look closely at the built in shelves in the living room you will see a few self-help books mixed in with the books on travel, art, psychology and books from Oprah's Book Club. My apartment is the perfect mixture of a trendy loft and old art deco style. As you enter the kitchen, living and hallway toward my bedroom there are archways lined with brick. The brick has this amazing color to them and it was the main reason why I rented the apartment. Well, one of the main reasons the other was the bar/pub downstairs from me. I have a weak spot for hamburgers and crispy French fries.

I cannot believe I did that to you. I went off there for a moment. What was I saying? I know I was making a statement about something. Not a statement but a point. Yes, now I remember. Sometimes I think that men are just as confusing as women because nobody knows what they want. People today are so scared to be independent and to be on their own. Both men and women are guilty of doing the same thing which is staying with someone for the sole purpose of not to be alone or thinking that since I've been with them for this long then it must be love or thinking that they will never find someone who suits them better because it's just too much effort. If all the people in the world settle, meaning that they never take a risk on someone or something, then how will they know what happiness truly is?

the architect

See, I did meet someone through the Internet, an architect/designer. His name was John and he was the one who initially wrote to me after viewing the profile I had written about myself. In the beginning we began with the typical conversations: What do you do? Where do you work? Do you enjoy what you do? How would you describe yourself? What do you like to do for fun? What are your interests?

You know what I am talking about, the

expanded description of yourself where you pull information together and try to show him that there is a common career goal or that there is a common interest among the things he likes to do. From there the dialog picks up and the humor that makes you who you are starts to shine through. You play little jokes on each other. Like when he says, "I am not a very good dancer but I will get out there and shake a little for you." You respond with, "That's okay, besides I hear they make special shoes now for people who have two left feet." You try to be cute and witty by trying not to hurt their feelings.

Now the only problem that can occur during the first conversations through the Internet is when you do not disclose a picture of yourself from the beginning. For some of us we want someone who is going to like us for what we represent on the inside because physical beauty can only take you so far in life. So I figured that it would be better not to post a picture of myself. I am an attractive woman. I usually give myself the cuteness award because I am not gorgeous but at the same time I am not ugly. Here I will give the written description that I have given so many others:

I am five feet tall with blonde hair and blue/

green eyes. I have a petite body with good muscular tone from all the cardiovascular exercise that I do. And people tend to say that I am a cross between a Sarah Jessica Parker and a Meg Ryan.

So like I said, I am an attractive woman. When you don't display a photo this is the response you can get:

"You've got to have a photo up there...no photo...no looky!

This service is so impersonal as it is...and the photo just let's ya know right off the bat who your dealing with and if you find them remotely attractive. It is easy to like words and what other people think of themselves (which is surprising at times), but don't have to snuggle up to words right!"

"Well thanks for writing. If you have a photo please send it along. If you have multiple, even better! We can go from there. If you want to enter this world of online dating...you gotta go in full fledge."

So here I am, confident in whom I am and all these guys are concerned about is how someone looks. Well once you begin to receive an email like that it can become a real turn off.

To finish the story about what happened with the architect, well nothing. We were writing back and forth having a detailed discussion about every day for approximately two weeks. He seemed to be kind, honest, interested in what I do and we had a lot of common interests especially when it came to art. But he too kept pressuring me for a picture. I explained to him that I just did not have a recent photo and really did not have the time or the knowledge of how to scan a picture onto the site. So I offered him my phone number so he could at least hear the sound of my voice. But he refused to call because he felt uncomfortable without seeing a face. Now I actually felt he was being a bit of a jerk about the whole thing because I had never seen a picture of him.

In the beginning John informed me that he would send me a picture of him and had asked me do the same. But of course I told him I did not have any recent photos and from there we kept on writing to each other. The catcher seemed to come when I had called him on this tiny fact because I felt he was being unfair and unreasonable about the whole situation. I explained to him that if he was only concerned with how someone looks than he should not have taken the time to write and continue to write for that length of time. When you develop a relationship with someone whom you have not met but share similar interests with you still feel hurt when things do not work out. John even had the balls to tell me that he mentioned me to a friend of his who doesn't mind talking with or meeting people where he has no idea of what to except. I mean, what girl wants to be pawned off on someone else's friend let alone through an Internet dating service? So the very last email I had written to John enclosed a statement that hopefully will make him realize that physical beauty is not all it's cracked up to be. Well, it was John's loss because he will never know what he really missed, someone special.

I know everyone is probably thinking that I should have sent a picture to John but when it comes right down to it I don't think that would have solved anything. I mean, how can we explain all of those success stories we hear about, relationships where people have known each other for years as friends first before they realized they where meant for each other. Ladies if we found our male friends to be attractive right off the bat then we probably would not waste year upon year developing a friendship with them and in the meantime sit there hoping and praying for a miracle to take place. For some reason I feel men would look at it differently because: One, they're men and two, men tend to be attracted to all of their female friends. But honestly, in order for a relationship to really work there needs to be a friendship first before anything else can happen. Because without that friendship you are constantly searching for that missing piece that makes the relationship complete.

So ended my Internet search.

the dinner date

Since the Internet was no real help, I realized that love was not a click away and I decided to try the next best thing; a blind dinner date. I truly do not know what is worse; meeting someone on the street or having your friends set you up on a blind date. Sometimes I get the feeling that my friends really don't know me at all but on this particular night I felt for the first time they had done something right. This was the night where I met Frank.

I was invited to dinner at my friends Jen and

Spencer's loft in the city. I honesty had no idea that I was going to meet someone because I figured it was going to just be the usual crowd. As I dressed for Jen and Spencer's dinner party I figured, Why be boring? Why not dress up for the evening? I had been working out at the local gym more than normal and I figured looking sexy was definitely the way to go. The way I looked at it was if the guy was a complete dud then that wouldn't prevent other men from looking my way.

I started searching my closet for the sexiest outfit I could find. I was standing in front of my full length mirror holding up different tops and bottoms, posing saying, "Hi, my name's Kelby," giving a little smile a twirl of hair a little giggle and letting my blue/green eyes sparkle.

Before I left the house I looked once more in the mirror giving my final approval. Black leather pants, little white silk halter top, two and a half sling back high heals, big sterling sliver hoop ear rings, a one of kind designer necklace that fell into my cleavage line, perfectly straight blonde hair and the make-up of a movie star. "You look good, Kelby," I said to myself. "All men beware, I'm coming out."

I looked over at the clock and it was already

ten past eight and I was running late. I grabbed my purse and keys and out the door I went.

Jen and Spencer have been married for about four years now and they just love playing matchmaker. So being the chosen single female of the group, every chance they get I become their little project. In the past the guys they bring over for dinner for me to meet have been the complete opposite of what I would date. But I always remember that you should never expect the unexpected because one day someone will surprise you.

As I turned to shut the door to the taxi, I looked up the sidewalk stairs in front of Jen and Spencer's brownstone and sighed.

New York is known for its brownstones. There is something about a brownstone that makes it one of the most attractive houses there is. The stucco has that rough edge finish while ivy entangles its corners giving the structure a gentle claming look. The apartment I live in is nothing compared to Spencer's family brownstone. About a year ago Spencer's father died of cancer and his mother just couldn't bare the thought of living alone so she moved down to Florida with some of her friends. Spence had no desire to sell the house. So he and Jen had the place updated and moved in a couple of months ago.

As I pressed the door bell I kept saying to myself, "Remember, Kelby, it's a night out so smile and have fun." In other words, don't let anyone put you down because you are still single. So I reached within myself and grabbed a hold of some courage.

The normal hugs and kisses took place and then came the introductions. Since I pretty much knew all the other couples there, there was going to be only one uncomfortable introduction. Before Jen introduced me to Frank, Steve came up to me and whispered, "You look amazing tonight."

Steve has been my best friend since high school and yes we dated which ended terribly because he decided to go after another girl while still dating me. Steve hurt me. It's because of his betrayal that I have never really forgiven him. Steve recently got married to a woman who is eight years older than him and to a woman he really does not love. Their relationship is strange. It's the type of relationship you find most people in. They settled for each other. They met in college and become comfortable with each other. He figured the next thing to do was to marry her especially since they had been together for seven years.

Steve believes that we will be married one day because I am the one who holds the key to his heart; not his current wife. I don't want to believe him but at the same time it's always hard to let go of your first love especially when he seems to still want you.

I should give you a little background information on Steve and myself. We grew up together and yes, in high school we dated. He was my first really bad breakup and probably my first real love. But to this day we have remained friends, best friends. When I went back to school to get my doctorate in California, Steve had become engaged to his current wife. While I was in California, he came out to visit eight months prior to the wedding to see if I had any feeling for him. I did not realize it then, but Steve wanted me to tell him not to get married. I never did tell him. I was so wrapped up in finishing graduate school that I could not picture myself getting involved in such a relationship. So ever since the day after his wedding, Steve has been making comments about how I am the one that holds the key to his heart.

I feel for Steve's wife, standing there in her

plain clothes. No makeup. No outgoing personality. Standing there sipping her wine and thinking, I married him and he is never going to leave me because he knows how helpless I am without him. To this day I think she only has hatred for me even though Steve says she has none. But women can tell these things and if your man was flirting with another women right in front of your eyes, wouldn't you feel some type of hatred?

Jen pushed everyone aside and brought Frank over to meet everyone, just in case he hasn't been embarrassed enough. Spencer first introduced Steve and his new wife and then came me. Spencer made it known that I was indeed the single one out of the group by using what he calls a sense of humor, while I began to wonder where was the door.

Frank was good looking. He was similar to Andre Agassi with that short shaved hair cut and black v-neck sweater over a pair of blue jeans. Frank worked with Spencer as a computer consultant in the city. He seemed witty which only made him more attractive to me. So with a martini in one hand and a good looking single man in the room, I began to wonder what was going to happen next. But honestly all I could feel was Steve's eyes on me while I was admiring Frank.

We all sat down for dinner. This was Jen's first time cooking Indian food. And instead of everyone asking me embarrassing questions they directed them toward Frank. As I sat across the table from Frank I could see his cheeks turning red and sense he was becoming very nervous. At that moment I really felt for him.

Everyone hates those types of questions, you know questions like: "When did your last serious relationship end? Are you dating anyone right now? It must be so hard to be alone?" For years my friends have tortured me with questions like these. And on that night all I wanted to do was shout out loud, "Stop you guys. It's enough already," and grab Frank's arm as we headed out the door letting it slam shut behind us. But that was only the voices in my head speaking. In reality I just sat there eating my food occasionally lifting my eyes up to see the expressions on Frank's very red face.

Once dinner was over I helped Jen in the kitchen cleaning up what mess was left. Jen said, "So, Kelby, what do you think of Frank. He pretty handsome isn't he?"

"Frank seems very nice. I just wish Spencer

had not asked him all those questions at dinner. I mean, the poor guy. He really is going to think we are all nuts."

"Kel, Frank knows Spencer was kidding around. Besides, I think Frank likes you; I can tell."

How could Jen tell? She been married for four years now and has not been out there. She has not seen the types of guys that are out there in the bars or clubs. Jen is very lucky because she did marry one of the few decent guys out there. But there are times when I wonder what Jen saw in Spencer because at times he can have a weird sense of humor.

Once Jen and I finished in the kitchen we went out to the living room where everyone had gathered. There was lots of talking and laughing going on as we entered. Spencer came up to Jen and me and informed us that everyone had decided to go out to a local jazz club for some after dinner drinks and dancing. "Everyone wants to go hear this great jazz player over at the Blue Note. Frank, what's this guy's name again? Anyway Frank says he is only playing tonight. What do you girls say, are you in?"

"Spence, it sounds like fun," Jen said.

Wow, a night at the Blue Note Jazz Café and

Club. The Blue Note has always been known to host the best of the best in jazz. Why, BB King is known to be a regular performer there. Frank liked jazz music. That was when I started to think that maybe my friends finally got it right, in picking a guy for me. We all grabbed our coats and headed down the steps of the brownstone to flag down a couple of cabs to take us over to the Blue Note.

As the first cab pulled up to the brownstone, Frank took my hand in a gentle way and pulled me into the cab. He told the cab driver where to go and that's when the one-on-one conversation began. The first conversation where you can either impress him or show him what a complete geek you really are. But once I saw his incredible smile up close, I began to think this is the guy and that anything I say could not be misconstrued as silly or foolish.

We arrived at the Blue Note Jazz club and the line outside was around the block. Thank God we knew the bouncer who always lets us in. Once we entered I heard Jen calling our names and signaling for us to come down to the main floor where there was a table waiting for us. Spencer ordered the drinks as the music entered our soul. It's very unusual for me to just sit still as the music fills my entire body. So I stood up and asked if anyone wanted to dance. Frank stood and took my hand as he led me to the dance floor.

He was so graceful on the floor. It was like a dream come true. Dancing so soulful with a handsome man and feeling like for the first time my friends had fixed me up with a real winner. But if that was the case then my story would end right there.

After dancing we went outside to grab a cab. During our cab ride back to my house, Frank asked me about Steve's relationship with his wife.

"Steve is an interesting guy but when I saw you interacting with him I thought you where his wife. You two seem to have much more chemisty. What's there story?"

"What can I say, but they settled for each other? Steve and I are just friends. He tends to flirt with all of his female friends." I tried to pretend that was Steve's normal behavior.

"Oh. But his wife, doesn't she see he doesn't love her. I guess it's just another divorce waiting to happen. It's just sad."

"Yes it is."

We returned to our previous discussion about how he wanted to decorate his new apartment. Of course, I mentioned what great artistic taste I had. But it also helped that we liked Pottery Barn, West Elm and Crate & Barrel.

"Maybe I will have you come over to take a look at my place so you could give me some ideas."

"I would love too." Hopefully that wasn't too forward but after all the martinis tonight, anything else would have sounded corny.

Frank whispered into my ear, "I would like to call you sometime. Would it be ok if I got your number from Jen"? I replied with yes. Then he kissed me good night.

That night I laid in bed thinking about Frank and when I might get to see him again. Then my mind shifted to Steve. Why does he make me feel so uncomfortable at parties? And how come he only appears to be more interested in me when there is another potential man in my life?

Then I started thinking about how Steve blames me for not telling him how I truly felt about him. How he is always saying that if I had given him a "Yes" or any sign of a future when he came out to California to visit then he wouldn't have gotten married. But all I can remember is how confusing of a time it was for me during graduate school.

I couldn't see that far ahead into the future, let alone tell someone not to get married because I still loved them.

A couple of days went by before I heard from Frank. My heart skipped a beat because I suddenly felt as if my luck was going to change for the better and that those lonely Saturday nights where going to be filled with Frank's presence.

The conversation over the phone flowed as if we had been friends forever. He made me feel comfortable in a way I had never felt before. You know, when you feel secure and how anything you say or do is seen as cute or adorable? That was the feeling I was beginning to get from Frank. But at the same time it scared me. Scared in the sense that I did not want to lose control over a guy I had only met a week ago.

Frank suggested that we get together Friday night for some drinks and dinner and whatever else would come out of the evening. I suggested going to a small Italian restaurant that a friend of mine managed. But that was going to be the first mistake of our first date.

My friend Michelle was managing this little Italian restaurant on the upper west side. For the past month, Michelle kept telling me to stop by for a drink because it had been so long since we had seen each other last. Michelle is one of those interesting friends whose personality can go from cute and funny to down right annoying. The annoying personality or better yet the depressive side always seems to come out when she breaks up with someone or she has gotten into an argument with her ex-husband, which can be a little problem when you are on your first date. From the moment we got to the restaurant to the time we left it was if there was an extra body sitting there with us fading into the background unloading all her problems. This happened to be the wrong night to visit Michelle let alone bring a date. A first date. At one point Frank asked her to please leave so we could at least enjoy our meal while I tried to recover from my everlasting mistake. But Frank just smiled and I became more infatuated with his presence.

Frank suggested that we head out to a local bar around the corner from where I live so we could finally spend some time together without being disturbed by annoying people. Our conversation was flawless. And I became captivatived. The music in the bar seemed to fade away and the people around us disappeared into the rustic walls that surrounded us. Frank had been the man I was looking for but I was waiting to see if he had a flaw. I did not want to believe he was perfect because I knew there was no such thing as perfection.

Frank walked me back to my apartment and I asked him in. As we walked into the apartment, I began to lead him into the living room and before I got to the couch, Frank grabbed my hand bringing me close to him and kissed me ever so softly. As we kissed, the passion from his mouth echoed into mine.

Even after our evening of great conversation and passionate kissing, there was no Frank after that. I honesty do not know what went wrong with Frank. Maybe it had to do with choosing a restaurant where an annoying friend just couldn't get the hint or maybe there really was no chemistry. My black cloud had returned. And so the "one dater" name became my topic of conversation. Well, at least it makes for a good laugh at Jen and Spencer's dinner parties.

go west young man, go west

Lately I have been thinking that this black cloud that is encircling itself over my head will one day swallow me whole. After all the mistrials and just meeting the jerks of the world I fear that I will never break this cycle. Ok, yes maybe I am supposed to go on all these one daters but it's beginning to put a damper on my self-esteem. If I hold such great qualities, have an attractive figure and have a good job then why aren't men throwing themselves at me? I have decided that men are just as confusing as women. Recently a friend told me that the reason why I am having problems with dating is simply because men are defected. She said that men are missing that extra chromosome off of the Y chromosome and that the missing piece went right to a part of their body that needs no real introduction. I could see her rational, but then why date? Well, being the optimist that I am, I put that explanation into the back of my mind and continued on with the dating saga I faced.

It wasn't too long before I met someone else. His name was Nate and he was a resident at a Hospital in Greenwich Connecticut. I just happened to be visiting my parents for the weekend and I thought it would be nice to do a little window shopping. Greenwich always did have great stores and restaurants plus if I had not walked into the Starbucks I would have never met Nate.

Nate's appearance was the first thing that drew me to him. He had a look about him. Almost mysterious. Like a Clark Kent because when he would put on his glasses he would look like a scientist and if he wasn't wearing them he looked so handsome. I must say even to this day Nate had all the qualities I would want in the opposite sex and his tall lean muscular body just made him out to be the perfect fit. I am not trying to sound superficial but we cannot forget that physical attraction does play a small part when we look at the opposite sex.

Everyone always told me that I should try to find someone who has a profession similar to mine or a profession that requires a high level of intelligence. Well, I figured I had it covered because here was someone who was not only intelligent but very good looking as well. Now I am not saying that only intelligent people will date other intelligent people. When I attended grad school I never thought about dating one of my classmates or someone in the same school because most of the guys where so conceited that it actually made you want to prove them wrong, let alone date them. I just figured it couldn't hurt to find someone who shared that similar commitment or knew what it was like to have to work hard in grad school. In a relationship, it's nice if the other person can understand what you are going though instead of questioning the reasons why you choose your profession. Where were all the supporting men anyway?

When we first met there was immediate conversation because he had grown up in southern California and did his medical schooling at UC Davis. So we talked about our memories of California and what we missed most about the area. As always the conversation over the hot tea was as normal as one could expect but there was a sense that the words I was saying were nothing but air.

Have you ever gotten that feeling from another individual that when you are talking they are thinking "la, la, la…who cares." Well, during my coffee house conversation with Nate I began thinking that very thing.

As we sat across from each other in those comfortable Starbuck's chairs, I kept thinking, If I could only hear what he was thinking. Did he like me? Did he think I was a total fool or idiot? Did he like what I was wearing and it went on from there? It was like I was obsessed with knowing what others thought of me. But I never cared what the world thought of me or cared for that matter. It was like all this rejection I had been getting was finally going to my head.

Once I readjusted my thinking from myself to what Nate was saying, he began to mention how he would like to do the rest of his residency at Mt. Sinai hospital in New York.

"Nate, that truly sounds great but would you want to move into the city or would you continue to live in Greenwich?"

"I would probably stay out here and commute into the city but I still have not decided yet."

"Do you go into the city a lot? What I mean is do you have friends in the city or family?"

"No family out this way. Everyone is still in California and I do miss them. For Thanksgiving I went to a friend's apartment in the city. He lives right off of fifth ave and I got to see the whole parade. It was really quite spectacular. Where abouts in the city do you live?"

"Down in the village. On the west side. I can not believe you went to the parade or I should say got to see the parade. This year I went up to my parents' house for thanksgiving so I watched the parade from their television set. But at least I had the best seat in the house."

"Kelby, when we where talking before it just dawned on me that I recently read this article in New York magazine and you might find it of some interest considering it talks about your field of work."

"I appreciate the information."

"Listen, I do not mean to cut this short but I need to run. I have to finish this case study before presenting it tomorrow morning in front of the chief of medicine. You know how it is. But I have your card and maybe we could get together again."

"I would really like that Nate. Besides I have to meet some friends later for dinner anyway."

And with a hug goodbye, Nate walked out the door.

After the coffee shop, I went home. While I was on the train heading back into the city, I thought to myself that he could be a good possible candidate. Now I started treating all men as possible candidates figuring it was better than getting my hopes up too quickly and then feeling disappointment when things go sour.

As soon as I opened the door to the apartment I could hear the phone ringing in the kitchen.

"Hello."

"Hey Kel, it's me." Me was Steve. Steve and I still maintain a very open relationship which lately I am wondering if that truly is a good thing when it comes to having a friendship. See, he is the one person I tend to talk to about all my guy problems. It's great to have a friend who is a guy because then you can begin to understand the male mind. That's if you choose to.

"What's up?"

"Just wanted to check in and see how things are going." He is always checking in with me. I guess he figures one day he will call and ask the same question and I will respond with I am getting married.

"Everything is good. And while I was up at my folks in Connecticut, I met the cutest medical resident from California at Starbucks in Greenwich. Listen I have to go. I have a very big day tomorrow and I just walked in. Talk more later."

"So this is good news. Let's see if we can make it to a second date this time."

"Very funny, Steve."

"No seriously. I hope he calls. But I am telling you, you are a very unique person and it's going to take another unique person to realize that."

"I know I am special"

"Seriously though, you know how all of this is going to play out don't you. I will have finished my MBA and have become very successful in my job and have been divorced for four years and had two years of therapy and then you and I will start dating again."

"Steve, I will be forty-eight by the time this all happens. Besides, I am not sure if I would want to date you. Listen I have to go. I have a big day tomorrow and I just walked in. Talk to you later."

"Sure. Have fun dreaming about your medical hunk."

"Very funny. Goodbye, Steve." And with that I hung up the phone and got ready for bed.

It wasn't too long before I received an email from Nate stating that he has decided to move back to California within the year and really did not see any reason to get involved with anyone at the time. Nate also went on to say that I was a beautiful and intelligent individual but starting any long term relationship would be definitely out of the question. As I read his email I kept thinking, Ok, I am beautiful and intelligent so what's the problem and when did we talk about a relationship? All I was thinking was let's have dinner first and see where things go. But I did not let this one get away that fast. So I wrote him back. The email read this:

> Nate, I honestly do not know where all of this is coming from because after you left all I was thinking was here's a guy who I might be able to become friends with. And what made you

> think I wanted a long term relationship? All I was thinking of was dinner. And where in the conversation did you mention moving back to California because from you said you wanted to do your residency at Mt. Sinai in New York? So if you plan on dating anyone out here, you better not because obviously you have plans to go west.

After I sent my response and had some time to dwell over the situation I decided to call Steve. This was probably not the wisest of choices but nonetheless we all can't be perfect.

"Hey, it's me. Did I catch you at a bad time?"

"I always have time for you, my love." My love? Was I truly Steve's love or was he just toying with me as always? This is why it is hard to be friends with Steve. He is consistently flirting with me. He flirts with me over the phone and in person and sometimes I feel wrong about being his friend. But at the same time he happens to be the one person who knows me the best.

"Steve, not now. Listen, do you think I'm cursed or something?"

"What do you mean?"

"What I mean is why do I keep meeting these

guys and nothing. It's like one date and then nothing. Dead end."

"Kel, you know you are a unique person and it's going to take another unique person to see that. Besides, you know one day you and I will end up together. Of course, that will be after my divorce, after I have had approximately two years of therapy because I don't want to come to you broken, and after I have had a meaningless affair. Then I will be yours." Sounds great, doesn't it?

"Steve, don't start with all that. I'm not in the mood. Besides I know how much you fear having a relationship with me. How it will ruin our friendship or how it will affect your abilities to be able to provide for me. But we are getting off the topic at hand. Steve, why have I become a one dater?

"Honestly, I don't know. You are the girl every guy dreams of and talks about to his friends. Maybe they know they are not the one for you. Try not to get down about this."

"How are things with you?"

"Same old, same old. But we can talk about that another time."

"Your wife's there, isn't she?"

"Yes," he said.

"I should go away. It's late and I'm starving. I think I'll order a pizza, perfect comfort food.

"Don't go nuts. Listen I'll call you tomorrow just to make sure you are ok."

"I'll be fine."

"I know but I'm going to call anyway. Listen have a good night."

"Thanks, Steve, for being a good friend."

"Anytime. Love you," he said softly into the phone.

"Love you too."

I hung up the phone thinking that I will always love Steve but my head tells me I should put an end to this fantasy he has of us being together. But it's my own fault that I continue to allow it to be what it is, a comfort knowing he is my fall back guy.

the olympian

So here the story continues and it continues on to the next idiot that walked into my life or better yet wrote into my life. Well, like I had mentioned before I tried the whole Internet dating world and now I thought I would give it one more try. Then you run into someone who just throws you for a loop and I don't mean that in a good way. But I was hoping that things would not continue as they had meaning one date and that's it. Well, this time there really was no real first date but I'm getting ahead of myself. Here's what happened.

I had finally posted my picture on an Internet site, not something I truly wanted to do but with all the insecure men out there not wanting to believe in a female's description you tend to just play along. So once the photo was up, there was a sudden increase in the amount of men who wanted to talk to me. The main reason why I did not want a photo of myself up on that dating site was I did not want men writing to me because they thought I had beautiful eyes or an incredible smile. Besides who wants to get hit on through a computer. Yes it's nice to see if there is an instant attraction but that's only about five percent of what makes a relationship really work. Only people who are truly shallow and consumed with the outer beauty of someone tend to believe that a relationship can be built on physical appearances only. I think women understand a little bit more about what I mean because when you see a good looking guy in a bar or club and then he opens his mouth and out comes nothing of true substance you automatically become turned off. Sorry about sounding like a therapist, it just comes out some times.

Now that the photo was up, the guys that

started to show interest in me were more the opposite of what I ever wanted in the opposite sex. So here I began carefully scrolling through their profiles and their initial email saying hello trying to decipher which one was truly unique and real. Then I received an email from one individual that seemed to catch my eye because he was trying to figure out if what I said about myself was true. He presented a challenge and knowing me I can not refuse a challenge. In the subject box of the email he wrote the words "clarification." Right away I was curious.

His profile described him to be a competitive athlete who had been to the Olympics (a wrestler I might add), looking for someone who understands what it means to be a competitive athlete and he went on to mention that he is a one-woman-guy. He also described that he was looking for that all-American girl, fourth of July American girl, a cheerleader type of girl. Now, when a female reads something along those lines you wonder what is he really looking for? The poster girl of the month? Well I did not understand why he was writing to me because I am not the cheerleader type; I am the complete opposite because I am a professional, intelligent, hardworking woman. I just happen to have an attractive body image. Well, after I read his profile, I clicked onto his picture to see what this guy looked like. Ladies, I have got to tell you he was gorgeous. But here's the problem, the picture was strangely cut and the pose the guy had was very seductive which made me truly wonder if this picture was real or not.

Let me describe the picture for you so you can get an idea. You see him lying there on his back on some type of bed or platform with one arm laced across his muscular lean pectorals and the other was bent back under his head. I mean, you see this and you think "oh god" and you start waving yourself with a fan. But the picture looked too fake. Like he had gone and cut it out of a Ralph Lauren catalog. So I figured lets continue on because you never know. I began to read the email which said, "So how does someone at age thirty-two become a doctor? Is the writing on your diploma still wet? If you want to response then here's my direct email address and my name is D." D stood for Dominick.

I wrote:

> Hi D-
> Let's start off an introduction. My name is Kelby, Kel for short. I do have a medical degree.

> One that makes me analyze your thoughts and tone of your initial email. And, no, the writing on my diploma is not still wet.
>
> So, I looked over your profile and you expressed that you are looking for someone who is an athlete or understands the commitments of an athlete.
>
> What sport did you play or currently play? I am sorry to cut this short but I need to go, just one question. Really why are you an Internet dating service? Why haven't you meet someone already? But you are probably wondering the same about me. Bye for now...
>
> Kelby

D wrote back the same day and said:

> Hello Kelby-
> Thank you for your in-depth response. Before we go any further you have to tell me if you are currently involved with anyone, that's not my style and I'm careful who I associate with especially women. Anyway if you are available you can give me a call. Have a nice day.
>
> -D

I proceeded to respond to his comment about if I am still single but I did not understand why that was a question. I mean if I was not single then why would I still be on an Internet dating site? Do people really do that, try to date as many people at the same time?

> D-
> No, I am not currently involved with anyone nor do I have men lined up at my door waiting for me to choose one of them.
> Kelby

Right away I got the feeling that this guy was very insecure. I called the number he had given me and there was no answer so I left him a message with my phone number. The first time he called me I did miss his call as well, so I wrote the next day saying how sorry I was that missed his phone call. In the message he left me, he made a comment about giving him my cell phone number so in the email that I wrote, I tried to explain that the cell phone is the best place to reach me with my busy schedule.

D responded with this:

> Hi: no problem my schedule is pretty full also, the cell phone thing was a joke, and you did sound very polite in your message to me. Contacting me is like Russian roulette you

> never know what will work but I have your number and I'll find you. Have a nice day
>
> -D

That evening we finally spoke over the phone. D had a very deep voice which led me to believe that he was Italian but he had a very heavy New York accent like someone out of a mobster movie. D pretty much dominated the evening's telephone conversation with his list of questions to see if he had me pegged all along. He was trying to find out if the picture of the girl he had seen matched the idea of this All-American girl that he created in his head. A petite blonde, with blue eyes whose virtue could take her straight to heaven. His line of questioning seemed to be along the lines of a truth or dare game to find out how innocent I was.

Now if I wanted to play games or twenty questions then I should have asked him for an application and asked him where I could send it. I don't know, maybe this was his way of getting comfortable with someone new. But seriously, nobody likes to talk to someone over the phone when the whole conversation is comprised of questions. With all the other men I have met though an Internet dating service, I have always had at the very least some form of an actually conversation. There have been only two guys that I have gone out with (only once mind you) where the conversation conducted was filled with questions. It's fine to have questions but when the questions seem more like a check list then that's when the problem arises. A checklist designed to see if your qualities match what they want in another individual.

But like everything, I ignored the voices in my head saying that this guy seems to be a little bit on the strange side. The only comment that truly bothered me was when he would say "Easy there, tough guy." I mean, what is that? Who talks to a woman like that? I felt like he was talking to one of his sports buddies or something along those lines. But the strange part was when he would say that comment. Here's a perfect example, D would say, "So, what sports did you play or do you still play now?" I told him I have played basketball back in high school and was a point guard. Then he would say, "Easy there, tough guy." Followed by "Really, you are sure you are not just messing around with me?" I suddenly got the feeling that what ever I was saying he did not believe me. What good does it do to not tell the truth when trying to use the Internet as a means to meet someone? So we said your goodbyes or goodnights rather and we hung up. The next day I thought I would just write an email saying that it was nice to have spoken on the phone. I thought it would be a nice little friendly gesture.

> D-
> Hi or good morning, I should say...I just wanted to say hi and say how nice it was to finally speak to you over the phone. When I left you a message last night I almost thought we were about to start playing phone tag but thank God we didn't. I hope that we can continue to get to know each other better because you seem like the kind of person who would make a good friend. I need to go but I will speak to you soon. So bye for now...
> Kelby

When in doubt always throw the friends line in there because then it shows them that you are looking for someone who can make a good friend as well.

D wrote in response to my email:

> So we are going to just be friends? You do have a sweet voice. I'd love to hear it whisper

in my ear sometime if you know what I mean.
Talk to you later

-D

Case in point ladies, the man only has a one track mind. See, a true gentleman would have written back saying how he too believes that the foundation for a good strong relationship is one that is built on friendship, love, understanding and respect. Ok, maybe in some unrealistic world they would say that. Did D honestly think he was being cute or was it his ill attempt at being romantic?

Again, the same thing happened when we spoke on the phone the next evening. He told me that same stupid line again, "Easy there, tough guy" or his little variation on it, "Easy there, killer." I mean, did this work for him in the past with other woman or did he just figure that since I had blonde hair that I would not know any better? So the eyebrow became raised and the suspicion began to grow thicker. When you talk to someone, whether it's someone you are just getting to know or someone you have been friends with for a while, it's nice to know that the other person you are speaking to believes what you are saying. Because again D kept on questioning certain comments I had made. Comments regarding the sports I had played, the fact that I am in shape and the fact that I do understand the commitments of a competitive athlete.

I asked him why he did not believe me and he said it was because my picture did not show him any images of what my body looked like. The picture I had posted was an up-close and personal shot of my face; a very natural picture, a picture that gave them a sense that this girl is real and she is not hiding behind makeup or fashionable clothing. So here I am thinking that this guy has got to be joking. Just because I chose not to display a full body picture you are not going to believe what I say about myself. This guy must have had some girl do quite a number on him, for him to not be very trusting.

Now during our phone conversations D started to mention that he liked the fact that I was like a little nerd. But who in their right mind wants to be called a nerd by someone they are just getting to know? It's one thing to say that to your spouse of fifty years but to a complete stranger, I don't think so. It was really funny because I don't think D understood that I am not a nerd. I just happen to be very knowledgeable in my field but when it comes to other little known facts I am absolutely clueless.

D mentioned over the phone that he would like to meet and for me to pick a day that would work best for me. This at first I thought was very sincere. But due to his competitiveness he decided that we should play a game of basketball. Now I honestly don't recall how this all came about over the phone but I believe it had to do with his persistant comments on if I truly did play basketball in high school. And the fact that he has a hang up on playing women in basketball simply because a female once told him wrestlers could not play basketball. So I figured an innocent game could not hurt for the first encounter. But where would we play? He lived in New Jersey and I lived in New York City, so we would have to come up with a middle ground to play. I figured it was only fair. D said that if we played I would have to give him something if he won and if I won he would do the same. He figured that the item should be a t-shirt or sweatshirt from the college we had attended. I felt that was again a fair deal.

The next day I received an email from D which read:

> Hello Kel:
> My turn for a nice email. You are a little nerd but I think its adorable (you're like the band camp chick) but I really like you I mean really really like big time. My friends don't understand my choice in girls. They figure I would want the big chested blondes but that's not my style. I never got involved with girls at Minnesota State; I was busy with wrestling and I never wanted to get "stuck" there with some farm chick like in An Officer and a Gentleman. I'm like twice the size of you but I think we will really hit it off, your voice sounds like a thirteen year old but It drives me wild for you. I want to hear it everyday. Anyway have a nice day and I'll see you in a week or so.
>
> -D

When I read what he had written, I wanted to write back and say how I too would have assumed based upon his picture and description of what he was looking for that a cheerleader-like girl would have been his first choice all along. Why was this guy so interested in meeting someone who has brains when he was a true jock that taught physical education? See I describe the person that I would want to meet as someone with intelligence, wit and a sense style. So why was I still attracting the opposites of what I wanted?

I responded back with:

> D-
> Well, I am no farm chick by far that's for sure....I'm a city girl...who is going to have fun playing basketball with you on Saturday next week. So you were very focused in college; I am impressed. But thankfully you didn't wind up with a farm girl because then I would have not met you. I too was much focused but more so in graduate school but that just fits my nerd profile. I think you are incredibly sweet...so I will find you a good t-shirt, don't worry. So until next time bye for now...
> Kel

D wrote back rather quickly to say:

> Hey: can you imagine if you win I'll have to break down and beg you not to tell anyone. On a serious note I wasn't comparing you to a Minnesota resident I was more trying to tell you how few women I have been involved with. You have no idea what I've missed out on in life , either cutting weight , lifting, etc. And by the way I like the name Kelby.

> Have a nice day
> -D (if you cut my sweatshirt I'll kill you)

I knew that he was not comparing me to a Minnesota farm girl. I was just trying to be cute and silly but I guess he missed that clue. But what I did not like about what he had written was what he missed out on in life. What was he truly looking for? I may look innocent and have blonde hair but that does not mean that I am stupid. So the eyebrow became raised again.

After our last email on that Friday a girlfriend of mine was coming down for the weekend for a little nightlife fun in the big apple. I had spoken to D that night right before we had gone out and he kept on telling me to not get to drunk or fall all over some guy in a club. Here I am thinking, Does this guy know me at all?

The interesting part of the story came when I started wondering if I truly wanted to meet this guy if everything in my gut was saying it was a waste of my time. So the next day I decided to write an email explaining my concerns especially about meeting him in some park to play a game.

> D-
> Now before I say anything please understand where I am coming from in this message to you. The only problem I have with going to New Jersey to meet you and have a good time is that I am a little hesitant meeting someone I don't know in a park that I am not similar with. Maybe you have to be a woman to understand completely but it's just the way I feel. It's just when you are single and a woman and it comes to meeting someone for the first time you want to able to meet someone in a place that is at least comfortable to you. I still would like to get together but if this is something you can not understand than I am sorry to have disappointed you, so please don't be upset by this email.
> bye for now...
> Kel

I figure that the email I had sent was direct and to the point but at the same time I was questioning the person he is. Sometimes you just need to go with your gut and my gut was telling me not to go. I also figured that if he was going to change my mind about the type of person I already thought him to be, he could prove me wrong in his response.

D wrote-

> I'm not upset, but you are predictable. I knew you were going to wimp out. You should have told me you didn't want to come here. It's not that big of a deal. I'm not going to bite you. It's the same situation in park A or B. You are such a hypocrite to you tell me you hate when guys go on the Internet to find someone better than you but you also capitalize in your profile how you don't play games, etc. I can't believe I was holding out for you.
>
> -D

I think the email said it all. How can guys assume because we are not up to the challenge that we had no intention of following through in the first place? The dating world is hard enough and when you meet someone like D it becomes even more of an uphill battle. For everyone out there you know exactly what I mean. So where did all the nice guys go and when was it going to be my turn to meet someone?

the seal comes last

Have you ever wondered what life has in store for you or if the road you are on is, in fact, the right one? Every time I ask myself these same very questions I think about the poem by Robert Frost, "The Road Less Traveled." I think about whether or not I have indeed taken the road less traveled. I look at the people I have met along the way and I think about the part they have played in my life. But lately I have been thinking about one person in particular, a pen pal I had. Now this was not a childhood pen pal where your elementary school teacher told you to write to someone far away as a class assignment. No, this was much different.

I was 32 years old starting my career as a doctor, living back at home (in Greenwich, Connecticut) to make ends meet and having bad luck in the dating department. My bad luck stemmed from three unsuccessful relationships and a lot of blind first dates. So when December 2002 came I decided to plunge myself into my career by opening up my solo practice and I decided to let fate take control of my love life. At this point in my life I had tried Internet dating not because I was desperate to find someone but in hopes to meet someone with similar interests since the bar scene was getting old. Besides, I figured since my friends were doing such a terrible job at fixing me up that a computer couldn't do any worse.

Well, it was three days after Christmas when I received an email from a man named Dominick. The email read:

> Hello, I was reading your profile and you seem like a great person to spend time with. I'm from Darien, but I am currently working overseas. I'll be returning home shortly and when I do I will be attending culinary school

> in Manhattan. I have a talent to make people laugh and have a great time. I enjoy partying, the outdoors and snow sports. I'm very interested in meeting someone like you. I have pictures that I can send to you if you would like. I hope to hear from you soon.
>
> -Dominick

At first I did not want to respond to his email especially after all the disappointment I had encountered by using the Internet as a way to meet people. Since I started using the Internet, the last six months were nothing but a lot of first dates without any second date.

There was something different about Dominick's email. He had written that he was overseas and the curiosity bug in me wanted to know more. So I wrote back. His email back to me read:

> Hey Kelby,
>
> It's great to hear from you. I thought that your email was really sweet. Now let me tell you a little bit about myself. I grew up in Darien until I attended Norwich University in Vermont. I studied History and English for two years. I left school to join the Navy, because it was something I've always wanted to do. The Navy placed me in San Diego where I went through Navy Seal School. After

completion I was stationed in Virginia Beach at Seal Team 8. Right now my job has taken me to Kandahar, Afghanistan.

I have been here for 3 months and I have another 3 to go until I return to CT. I've seen a lot of bad things since I've been here yet I have also had the opportunity to see a beautiful country.

When I return from Afghanistan, I will be moving back to Connecticut probably to Stamford or Darien, CT. I have plans to attend the French Culinary Institute which is in Manhattan. I've always loved to cook and I have a real knack for it. I plan on opening my own restaurant in the future.

I also find that running is very soothing, it relieves stress as well as keeps me in top physical condition for my job. I always enjoyed running in the mountains when I was in VT, it really put me at peace. Along with running I am really into snow sports and the outdoors. I always find time to go snowboarding or camping because it's so much fun. I wonder if you ski or snowboard. I work really hard at everything that I do, and I've never quit anything that I've started.

I really enjoy talking to you Kelby; you are a great person with a lot of things to offer. I'm working on sending you some pictures

> online, be patient because I am busy here and there is a 9 1/2 hr difference.
>
> Take Care, Dominick

At that moment I felt an overwhelming desire to write again and again. That was the start of our friendship and for the first time in my life someone was going to know me first before deciding if anything romantic would come out of knowing the other person. So, at age thirty-two I became Dominick's pen pal.

Everyone always says that it is sometimes easier to talk to a stranger than to someone who really knows you. I look at my friendship with Dominick as a blessing because my life was about to change and Dominick needed a friend. To be able to give something to someone else without needing anything in return is the ultimate sacrifice you could give someone. What I gave Dominick was not something that I will ever forget, nor will he.

December 31, 2002:

New Year's Eve, the one holiday I was not particularly excited about celebrating because I did not have any plans or a date. The year before I threw a party with thirty people but this year it looked like no one wanted to invite me to their New Year's Eve party. But I did not really care. I figured it's all part of the bad luck I was experiencing. The only person who put a smile on my face was the one person who could not be here for New Year's Eve, Dominick. His email read:

> Hello Kelby,
> It's great to hear from you again. Yeah, the holidays are not the same when you are far away from family and friends, but someone has to be here. This place really isn't that bad. We've had some famous people visit us while we've been here. Robin Williams and David Letterman came to our compound and we all got to meet them and have our pictures taken with them. The weather gets pretty cold here so the holiday season doesn't seem so distant.
>
> Why did I become a Seal...well my father and grandfather were both in the Navy so it seemed like the traditional thing to do. The Seals go through the hardest training in the world and I wanted to be a part of that brotherhood. The guys that I work with are great and knowing that they would do anything for you, especially give their life for you, is unique. Most of the operations that we do go unnoticed and never come up on the news.

It doesn't matter though, all of us know the good that we do regardless of the recognition we don't receive.

That is great that you love to cook. I have yet to find a woman who enjoys cooking the way that I do. I enjoy it so much that I'm getting out of the Navy soon to become a chef. I have always believed that the way to a woman's heart is through her stomach...hahaha!

I'm also very happy that you to love the city. Most of my friends that I work with have never been to NYC. I tell them constantly that it is the best city on the planet and that they must go there sometime. I grew up going down to SoHo and Little Italy as a kid, it has so much history it's overwhelming.

You ask why Internet dating? Well, I haven't had a serious relationship in over a year because I've been on the road a lot and I really haven't found someone that I can connect with. Virginia Beach isn't really the ideal place either, but that's why I am excited to move back home in a few months. I figured that I would go online and see what kind of new people I could meet, so far it's been pretty successful. I'm curious why you have tried Internet dating as well?

That is great that you ski. I love skiing and snowboarding. It is a great way to relax and enjoy life. Me and a few friends are going up to Whistler in Canada when we return from our stay in Kandahar.

I have to get going; I'm cooking New Year's Eve dinner for my platoon. I really enjoy talking, you are very sweet Kelby. I look forward to talking to you and meeting you some day.

Take Care, Dominick

So my New Years Eve consisted of replying to an email, a couple of good movies and knowing that one day I would meet the person of my dreams.

That evening I fell asleep at ten o'clock in the evening and woke the following day with a renewed self-assurance because I could feel that this was going to be the year that everything came together.

January 1, 2003:

I woke to a very rainy New Year's day but my life felt in control. I went out that day and hit the stores because I needed a new image. You would figure with all the sales going on New Year's day that every female would be out shopping up a storm but to my surprise there was nobody out.

Maybe it was the rain or just maybe my luck was changing.

I had decided that if I was going to go out shopping that I was not going to go to the mall so I decided to shop on Greenwich Avenue. Greenwich Avenue had everything from Banana Republic to J Crew to Nine West to Tiffany's. I figured I would start at the top and work my way down. So as I turned onto Greenwich Avenue there was not a single car parked along the side streets or in front of the stores. It was only three o'clock in the afternoon so where could everyone be? I knew the stores were open but where are all the people?

So I pulled right in front of each store and claimed the store as my own for the entire hour I was there. Despite the rain, I was the happiest female shopper out there because I got sixteen new outfits for an incredible price and some where far away there was this person thinking about me and what I was doing.

The only question that wrestled in the back of my mind was, Why me? Here is this guy far away from home with no girlfriend and a lot of spare time on his hands when he was not out in the field, so why was he continuing to write me?

So I asked him and this is what he said:

> Why did I decide to write you, well you seem really nice and someone that I would like to meet. I forget what age I put down in my profile. I'll tell you that I'm glad that I wrote to you and look forward to meeting you when I get home.
>
> Dominick

It wasn't too long before I received an email from Dominick saying he was coming home. He assured me that this time there was going to be no delay in his return. Dominick had written me before saying he was going to be leaving the Middle East and then they (the Navy) would send him back out into the field on special assignment. He always hated that part of the job.

This time I said to myself, "Kelby, don't get your hopes up just yet."

Dominick said that when he got to Virginia he would email me and then he figured it would be another two weeks before he would be back in the big apple. He told me that if he could he would fly right to New York not back to the base. He said he had to still follow the rules and regulations of the

Navy but once he is discharged then its back to being a normal citizen.

I turned off my computer after writing Dominick back telling him that I was keeping my fingers cross. I looked up from my laptop while my fingers gently tapped the top of the computer and began to dream. The T.V. was on and I could hear the voices of the Today Show in the back round. I turned slightly in my chair. I stared at the T.V. I saw four couples talking to Matt and Katie about how they met. As I listened to their stories I thought about my story with Dominick. I pictured the two us standing there talking to Matt and Katie and the entire world about how we met and how we became pen pals in a sense first and then realized we where the perfect match after that first face to face meeting. My day dream was interrupted by the phone ringing.

"Hello"

"Hey, it's me. I didn't except to catch you at home. How are you?"

It was Steve. I hadn't spoken to him in awhile. I did not want him to know about Dominick and I wasn't in the mood for any head games. Nor did I want him to know that I had tried the Internet dating world again. It had been about a year since

I had spoken to Steve and I was pretty sure not much had changed with him. He was still married to a woman he really didn't love.

"Hi Steve. Sorry about not getting in touch with you this past year. I guess time flies when you're busy." Busy writing back and forth to someone who will hopefully find me attractive in person when he comes home in approximately a month.

"You know I just like to check in with you. Anything new going on with you?"

I had to be careful how I answered. "Nothing new. Just the same old. New patients everyday, working a little later then usual. Like I said, nothing exciting."

"Testo is playing at Shelter this weekend and I am putting some people together. Are you interested?"

"Maybe, I'll have to see. I may go up to Watch Hill Rhode Island this weekend to visit with my grandparents and I was thinking about going Saturday through Sunday. I'll let you know toward the end of the week," I said.

"I really need to go dancing and you know I love dancing with you. But keep me posted. Listen I'm at the office so I need to go. What time are you working today?" Steve said.

"I took the morning off so I could get some things done here. I plan on going in at ten today." I really did not want to talk to Steve this morning and I was trying everything to get him off the phone as quickly as possible.

"Ah, the benefits of owning your own business. I will talk to later."

"Bye Steve." I hung up the phone and took one last gulp of my coffee. I looked at the kitchen clock. Eight-thirty in the morning already. I've got to get going.

Approximately two weeks had past before I received an email from Domick.

The email read:

> Hi Kel. Sorry it has taken me this long to write but I am in Virginia. God, it's good to be back on American soil. Once we left it has been crazy here with all the debriefings. No down time at all. I am in process of being discharged and once that happens then its time to come home. Since I am now in the same time zone as you, let alone the same county, I was wondering if I could get your phone number so we could at least talk until we meet. I am looking forward to meeting you and who knows

> maybe I will even cook for you. I could make you an authentic Italian dish, one my grandmother taught me how to make. I am sorry to cut this short but they are calling for us to return to the conference room. I just wanted to write so you would know where I was and that I am home. Safe at last. Send me your number and I will try to call you in a couple of days.
>
> Dom

I quickly wrote back and enclosed my phone number. Picturing what he sounded like was the best thing. Wondering if he had a low voice or a deep voice and hoping he did not have a high pitched voice. Sometimes you wonder how someone who looks so handsome can have such an awkward voice.

Just about two days had passed when the phone rang.

"Hello."

"Hi, is Kelby there?"

"This is Kelby."

"It's so nice to talk to you finally. What's going on?"

"Dominick is that you?"

He did have the perfect voice. So far so good.

From his picture he was handsome and his voice only made him more attractive.

"Hi Kelby. Yes it's me and I am in person. Maybe not in person but getting closer."

"I can not believe I am actually talking to you. This is so unreal."

"It's nice to hear your voice. I want to thank you for writing to me all this time. You have no idea how much I looked forward to reading your emails each day."

"I am glad to hear you found my emails helpful. How are things in Virginia?"

"Things here are moving right along and it looks like I will be home in another four days. So do you have any plans Saturday night?" Dominick asked.

"You are going to be here? In Connecticut? This weekend? No, I do not have any plans this weekend." My heart was starting to race.

"Well, you do now. Why don't we meet up around 9:30 p.m. on Saturday? Any suggestions on where?" Dominick wanted to meet me. We were not just going to be pen pals.

"There is a place called the Loft in South Norwalk on Eighth Avenue and Houston Street. It's a small lounge/bar but they make really good drinks and there is always a nice crowd."

"Then it's all set. The Loft at 9:30 this Saturday. We have a date."

"It's a date." I was trying to contain myself over the phone.

"I need to go but we will connect this weekend," Dominick said.

"Yes, this weekend."

I hung up the phone and started thinking about what I was going to wear. It's all about the clothes now. That night I dreamed and dreamed about our first meeting and I wanted so badly for everything to go right. But this is a story where nothing appears as it seems.

Saturday night. I finished putting the finishing touches on my hair, reviewed the accessories, found my favorite hoop ear rings, and gave myself a once over in the mirror. Now let's see if Dominick likes me. I grabbed the keys to the house and headed out the door.

The loft wasn't too far from my house and it was a nice evening so I decided to walk. South Norwalk seemed so alive. And more important. I felt excited not nervous like I usually did when meeting someone for the first time. This was going to fun.

I showed my ID at the door and entered the loft. It was just a little bit after 9:30. Just a little late. I began looking around the place trying to spot Dominick. But no luck.

"You look like you are trying to find someone." I turned around and there was two guys standing next to me.

"I am meeting someone and I don't seem to see him." My heart felt crushed a little.

"Would you like to have a drink with us while you wait for your friend? Mike get the woman a..."

"Cosmo, thank you."

"A cosmo."

So there I was waiting but at least I knew I still had it. To this day I still do not remember those guys' names but I thank them for making me feel special or better yet, wanted. It was not until an hour later that Dominick showed up. He came up behind me and said he sorry about being late. I introduced him to my new friends and thanked them for the drink. Dominick and I headed over to a small table.

"Sorry about being late. I was having trouble with what I was wearing."

I'm sorry, did he just say it took him over an hour to figure out what he was going to wear? It's great to see a man take care of himself but this sounds a little much.

"That's ok. I've been having a nice time here while waiting for you."

"I see. Who are your friends?"

"I just met them tonight. They knew I was waiting for someone and they decided to keep me company."

"Oh, I see."

We sat and talked even laughed a little. There was nothing, no spark, no chemistry. Just two old friends catching up. Well, that's what it seemed. It was probably just a little after mid-night when I decided to call it a night. We left the Loft together and Dominick walked me to my car. Not much was said on the walk to the garage and I think we both knew the only relationship we were where going to have was going to be a friendship.

We arrived at my car and with a warm hug goodnight, I slipped into my car. I looked into the rear view mirror to only watch him walk away. In my heart, I know he was grateful for the time I spent writing to him everyday while on assignment in Iraq. But what my heart really wanted was to fall in love. Just like everyone else.

That ends my story for now but I will tell you that about three years ago I finally did meet someone. Someone special and my perfect match according to me.

But that's for another time and another story.